# Caboose

## the Pot-bellied Pig

Caboose, who lived in our kitchen,
thought she was a dog but eventually
learned to find her own true voice.

Merry Christmas, Marlenne!
2019

by Caroline Klemperer
illustrated by Nick Green

Caboose was a pig, a pot-bellied pig, who thought she was a German Shepherd dog.

Wherever Arlo went, she was there.

When Arlo barked, Caboose let out a **sqruff**.
When he growled, she **sqrowled**.

She slept by his side in the kitchen of the house.
They looked like one shadow in the corner of the room,
her bristly hide against his smooth dark fur.

When Arlo went for a walk, Caboose was close at his heels. When he came racing home, she followed behind as fast as her stubby legs could go.

At dinner, Caboose waited till Arlo had his fill, then she sauntered over to his bowl and gobbled any dog food he might have left behind.

Caboose also loved melon rinds and knew when they were left in the garbage beneath the sink.

One day she sneaked to the door, pried it open with a twitch and a wiggle of her nose and pulled all those delicious delicacies out onto the floor.

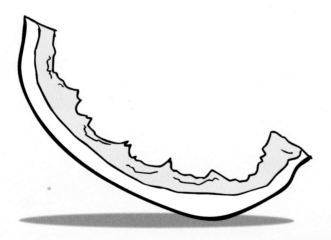

What a naughty pig.

The next day she tried another cabinet door, and with a wiggle and a twitch of her clever nose she opened that one and discovered cereal, then raisins and peanuts, pancake mix, pasta, and bananas.

Caboose was sent outside.

When the sun went down Caboose ambled back to the house and thumped on the door with her powerful nose, but no one came. She called to Arlo with her piggy bark, but he was already asleep.

Caboose lumbered back down the steps, her belly scraping against the warm rocks, and headed for the shed. There she settled into a pile of straw.

She was feeling lonely, thinking of Arlo and melon rinds and cereal, when something soft and gentle tickled her floppy ears. She heard a purring, then felt a wet tongue against her cheek.

Caboose pulled herself up onto her chubby legs and
waddled over to slurp some water from her pan.
The kitten pranced up and had a drink, too.

Caboose ran round and round the shed. The kitten scampered behind her. Caboose made a cave under the straw. The kitten crawled in after her.

Caboose lay down. The kitten lay down, too,
its soft gray fur against the pig's bristly belly.

"*Meow*,"
said the kitten,

and Caboose, content
and happy, replied,

"*Oink.*"

For Matthew, Aaron and Nicholas, who inspire my storytelling. —CK.

For all the stories that never made it into book form. —NG

Caroline Klemperer, violinist and writer, divides her time between New York City and a farm in Indiana where she spent her childhood and where she and her husband raised their three sons.

Many of the farm animals who, like Caboose, made their home in the family's kitchen, found their way into Caroline's picture books and children's programs.

Nick Green currently lives in Portland, Oregon, and has various creative endeavors involving computers, music and nerf herding.

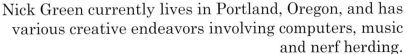

Chanticleer Publishers
Text copyright © 2013 by Caroline Klemperer
Illustrations copyright © 2013 by Nick Green
Layout design by Sarah Richardson Green
ISBN 978-0-615-79659-8